S.R. Martin

INSOMNIACS

TAL

SCHOLASTIC INC.
New York Toronto London Auckland Sydney
Mexico City New Delhi Hong Kong

ISBN 0-590-69142-2

12 11 10 9 8 7 6 5 4 3 2 1   9/9 0 1 2 3 4/0

Printed in the U.S.A.

First Scholastic printing, May 1999

CHAPTER ONE

The old Dixon house was not what you'd call inviting. It sat on the very edge of town, even though it had been one of the very first buildings in the area. It was almost as if the houses that had been built later on had been placed as far away from it as possible. No one knew why this was the case, but everyone accepted that it was so.

It had been that way for as long as anyone could remember, and parents still told their children not to go near the place, the same way that their parents had told them.

There was something about the house that inspired fear, a sense of something not quite right, though from appearances it was hard to tell why. It was an old Victorian-style place with a high slate roof covered in moss. If you peered hard through the rusting spiked gate that was set into the six-foot-high bluestone wall around the perimeter, you could see the wide porch that ran around the front of the place. There were several old wicker chairs here and there, some with rotting cushions still on them. The long windows that ran from the floor almost to the ceiling always had their yellowing lace curtains drawn, and sometimes late at night you could see a weak pale glow behind them, as if old Mrs. Dixon still lit the place by candle.

The trees around the house were massive, old oaks and elms, and a few pines that must have been there when the house was first built. Around them, in wild profusion, were azaleas and camellias and what appeared to be like an entire sea of ferns. The garden had overgrown itself time and time again, until it was a wild mass of greenery, so thick during spring and summer that it was almost impossible to see anything except the roof of the house. In winter, after the leaves had fallen, it looked like something from a nightmare.

Old Mrs. Dixon had also been there for as long as anyone could remember. In fact, Florea Low's mother could remember her mother referring to Mrs. Dixon as *old*, which to Florea was a curiosity in itself. How could anyone be old in her grandmother's day and still be old now? It just didn't make sense, yet when she asked her mother about it she was told not to ask silly questions.

Florea knew it wasn't a silly question, but

she also knew not to question her mother. Even though the Lows had lived in Knox since Florea's grandparents came from China, and Florea was about as Australian as anyone could get, at home there was still a lingering sense of tradition, and you simply didn't question your parents' instructions. Not if you wanted any kind of social life besides going to school over the next month or so.

Florea, however, was a very curious kind of girl. Exceptionally curious. And if her mother wasn't going to satisfy her questions, then Florea was the kind of person to go out and satisfy them herself. Because of this she was a straight-A student at school and had won several prizes for academics, though she did have the habit of getting into trouble on occasion when she felt her questions for her teachers hadn't been answered to her satisfaction.

So it was a combination of things that led Florea to the rusty gates of the old Dixon place late one wintry Saturday afternoon.

There was a slight breeze blowing and it moved the masses of fallen leaves around the house into drifts almost three feet high. The sound of them moving made it seem as if the house itself were hissing at her, making her roll her shoulders uncomfortably. It was a creepy place, there was no denying that, but it was still just a house. And the only living thing in there was a little old lady, so Florea knew there was nothing to be frightened of.

Nothing to be frightened of at all.

2 CHAPTER TWO

Florea had no idea what she was going to say to the old lady when she got inside, but that didn't bother her all that much. She was the kind of girl who found it easy to talk to most people and was sure that when the moment came, the right conversation would spring to mind.

The gates squealed slowly open on their rusty hinges, and as she stepped inside a sudden flurry of leaves blew around her legs, like the dried and discarded skins of long-dead creatures.

"I'm not frightened," she whispered to herself. "I'm not frightened."

The path up to the house was made of the same blue stones as the wall, sunk so far into the earth that only their top surface was visible. Her feet crunched softly on the covering of leaves and small sticks, and she had to occasionally push aside ferns that had overgrown the path completely.

When she made it to the house itself, the level of decay in the building became more obvious. The wide porch sagged at the edges, as if it had grown tired of keeping its end up all these years and had decided that a little droop here and there was nothing to be ashamed of. The ornate metal pillars that supported the roof had large sections of rust dribbling like bloodstains through the once-white paint. And the gutter had as many holes in it as preelection promises from politicians.

Old wind chimes softly sounded through the hissing of the leaves, and the naked branches of the trees creaked and groaned with age.

"Just an old house," Florea whispered. "One that's going to fall down soon, from the look of it."

"What was that, dear?" came a voice from off to Florea's left.

After she had settled back into her skin (something she'd jumped clean out of at the sound of the voice), Florea turned her very wide eyes in the direction the words had come from.

To begin with, she didn't see anything.

There were a couple of sagging chairs grouped around a three-legged wicker table, but no sign of anything that could conceivably move, let alone speak.

And the voice had been quite strong, nothing at all like what you'd expect from a little old lady who'd already been old when your grandmother was young.

"Excuse me?" Florea said in her tiniest voice.

"I asked you what you'd said," came the voice again. "Come over here where I can hear you better. My ears aren't what they used to be, and you have a very soft voice, child."

This time Florea made out what appeared to be a bundle of rags scrunched down in the corner of one of the wicker chairs, so deep in the shadows of the porch that they'd been impossible to see to begin with. A sticklike hand had magically grown out of the rags and was beckoning her over.

"Come on, dear," the voice continued, "come talk to me."

Hands behind her back, Florea shuffled up onto the porch and edged slowly along toward the source of the voice.

The closer she got, the clearer the figure in the chair became.

It wasn't much bigger than herself and its limbs were so thin they looked like bones with a little skin on them. The face was almost mummified and appeared to have no flesh on it at all. A pair of pinprick eyes stared out from among a straggle of wispy white hair.

Mrs. Dixon was swathed in so many layers of clothes she could have been one of the homeless people Florea had seen when she'd visited the city once with her parents. There were sweaters and shawls and cardigans, and around her shoulders an old woolen blanket.

"That's better," the voice continued as Florea came closer. "Now you can talk to me."

Mrs. Dixon's voice was like thick honey. Florea could feel it flowing through her ears like liquid gold, coating her brain with a rich brightness that made her feel warm and comfortable.

"Sit," the voice commanded, and Florea took the ratty chair next to the old woman.

The sticklike hand snaked out from the rags and clutched Florea's arm, and even though it felt as if she had been grabbed by a skeleton, it didn't seem to bother her all that much, not as long as she could hear that beautiful, rich voice that filled her with such a feeling of well-being.

"Isn't this cozy?" said Mrs. Dixon.

When Florea finally left the house, she had no real idea of how long she'd been there, though it must have been quite some time because the streetlights had come on in town.

She wandered toward her home, feeling a little light-headed but happy, as if she'd spent a wonderful summer's day chatting with old friends. The odd thing was, Florea actually had no idea what she'd talked to old Mrs. Dixon about, though she had to have talked an awful lot because her throat was a little hoarse.

As she walked, the memory of that strangely rich voice filled her with such a sense of well-being that she did a little leap into the air and clapped her heels together.

What a lovely old lady, Florea thought. How on earth could anyone be afraid of her? And why does everyone say not to go near the place? Mrs. Dixon's as harmless as a newborn calf.

However, when she finally walked through the door into the kitchen at home and saw the look on her mother's face, Florea decided it probably wouldn't be a very good idea to say where she'd spent the afternoon.

"Where have you been, young lady?" her mother asked. "You're over an hour late for dinner. I was thinking of calling the police."

"Oh, just wandering around," she replied, her face flushing hot as the lie slipped past her lips.

Then she started sneezing.

3 CHAPTER THREE

$\mathcal{T}$he next morning, Florea had one doozy of a head cold. Her sinuses were blocked with snot, her eyes were watering, and every time she opened her mouth a sneeze exploded from it with enough force to shoot her head back on her shoulders.

"I'd love to know what you were up to yesterday, young lady," her mother said as she squinted at the thermometer she took from Florea's mouth. "Your temperature's shot right up and you seem to have developed the cold from hell overnight."

"I was just wandering around thinking, Mom," she replied, but it came out more like, "I wab jumb wannerin awoun binking, bob."

"Well, the only wandering you're going to be doing for quite some time is from your bed to the bathroom, and that's it. I don't want this developing into pneumonia. You are not to get out of bed unless nature is calling very loudly."

"Yes, Mom," Florea moaned.

It was a gray Sunday outside and the windows to Florea's bedroom were sprinkled with tiny drops of rain.

Her head was blocked solid and her face felt swollen and disgusting. Every time she took a breath it felt as if her chest were on fire, and the sneezes got so bad they started to lift her off the mattress and into the air.

A nice day for staying in bed, she thought as she turned over and snuggled back down under the covers.

It must have been, because Florea didn't wake up again until well past lunchtime, and lunch was something Florea had hardly ever missed in the entire time she'd been on the planet. She was a person who had a fairly high metabolism and needed regular intakes of fuel in order to function at her best.

Next to her bed was a tray containing a couple of bologna sandwiches and a glass of milk. She stretched out her hand, surprised at how weak she'd become, and took one of the sandwiches. And even though she didn't really feel like eating, she forced herself to take a small bite. Then another.

And another, until everything was gone from the tray.

The food seemed to work wonders, and Florea found herself filled with a sudden excess of energy (and a very full bladder). A quick dash to the toilet later and she was in the kitchen, rummaging through the fridge under her surprised mother's gaze, trying to find any leftovers.

"That was a rather quick cold," her mom said. "Not that I'm complaining. At least you'll be okay to go back to school tomorrow, from the look of things."

Florea nodded in agreement as she devoured a cold sausage in a couple of wolflike bites and lunged back into the fridge to see what else she could find. It felt as if she hadn't eaten anything for weeks, and she kept snacking on and off right up until dinnertime, when she consumed a meal the size of which would have made a construction worker nervous.

"I wish we had more people with appetites like yours in the restaurant," her father said as he watched her polish off a second helping of roast chicken. "We could retire in a year or two."

Florea grinned and sucked the crispy skin and flesh off a leg.

"You finished eating, Dad?" she asked, eyeing the scraps on her father's plate.

He pushed it across to his daughter and stared wide-eyed as she scraped everything he'd left onto a thick slice of white bread and started shoveling it all into her mouth.

"I really love roast chicken," she mumbled around the huge mouthful of food. "We should have it more often."

Her parents looked across at each other. Both had confused frowns on their faces.

When Florea woke up on Monday morning, she had pretty much returned to normal, and ate an average-sized breakfast.

"Another helping of oatmeal?" her mother asked, holding the saucepan out to Florea.

"Thanks, but no thanks," she replied. "Anyone would think you're trying to fatten me up."

"You keep eating like you did yesterday and you'll end up needing a whole new wardrobe," her mother muttered.

"Yesterday?" Florea looked puzzled.

"When you cleaned out the fridge and then ate most of your father's dinner as well."

Florea scratched her head. "I don't remember."

"What? You don't remember eating all that food? There's no way you could forget. I certainly won't."

"No," Florea said, still scratching her head. "I don't remember yesterday."

"It must have been the aftereffects of that cold."

"What cold?"

Apart from the not-quite-twenty-four-hour cold and a sudden bout of memory loss, Florea was pretty much herself again and her mother sent her off to school like normal.

And everything progressed through the day pretty much as normal as well. Florea breezed through her classes, ate an average-sized lunch at pretty much normal speed, and performed quite well during the afternoon hockey practice. It was, however, while she was showering after gym that things started to get a little strange again.

She was madly soaping under her arms and whistling the melody from a new song she'd heard on the radio (the only words

27

that she could remember from it were "How bizarre, how bizarre"), when she heard a rich, warm voice quite distinctly say, "Talk to me."

"Pardon?" Florea said, turning to the girl next to her in the showers.

"Why? What did you do?" the girl replied, looking at Florea strangely.

"Didn't you just say something to me?"

"No."

Florea looked at the girl and the girl looked at Florea.

"Sorry," said Florea. "I must be hearing things."

The girl smiled and went back to showering, which was when Florea heard the voice again.

And she continued to hear it for the rest of the afternoon. No matter where she was or what she was doing, the voice seemed to insinuate itself, flowing like liquid gold through her senses.

The more Florea heard it, the less she heard anything else, until, when the final bell rang for the day and she packed her books into her bag for the walk home, she simply ignored the good-byes of her friends and wandered, glassy-eyed, from the school yard and off down the street.

"Talk to me. Talk to me," was all she could hear. It resonated through her body, making her skin tingle and her mind go pleasantly numb.

Instead of taking the direct route home, as she usually did, Florea wandered out to the edge of town until she came to the old Dixon house. Without pausing, she opened the gate and strolled up the path, a half smile on her face.

When she arrived at the porch, Mrs.

Dixon greeted her with a smile and patted the seat of the chair next to her.

"Come and sit here, dear. Come and talk to me."

When Florea sat down, the old woman's arm snaked out and her hand took hold of the girl's. There seemed to be a little more flesh on it than the time before, and the old woman's face had just a smidgen more color in it. Her eyes glinted strangely and a pink tongue flicked out and licked her razor-thin lips.

"I'm so glad you came back," said the honey-thick voice.

"Have I been here before?" asked Florea.

"Of course not, dear. And you won't ever have been."

4 CHAPTER FOUR

Florea's mother was starting to worry about her daughter.

Several times Florea had come home much later than normal, and each time she'd said the same thing: "I've just been wandering around thinking."

Now, Mrs. Low was not normally a suspicious person and she trusted her daughter implicitly, but she could tell when something was not right. Also, the fact that every evening after one of these "late spells" Florea would come down with an illness of some kind that usually lasted about twenty-four hours and left her extremely weakened and outrageously ravenous, was certainly cause for concern.

So far Florea had suffered from colds, mild food poisoning, an especially savage attack of diarrhea, and what the doctor had called an allergic reaction to water.

The other things that were bothering Mrs. Low were that these "late spells" were becoming more frequent and closer together, and that afterward Florea was always at a loss as to having been sick. She'd recover, eat like a couple of horses, and then look vague when either her mother or father mentioned the illness or her appetite.

And the final thing that really had Mrs. Low worried was the lying.

In all her years, and to the best of her

mother's knowledge, Florea had never told her parents a lie. Occasionally, she'd been a little selective about the truth, but she'd never told an outright lie. And Mrs. Low knew for certain that Florea was not telling the truth about where she went when she disappeared.

What brought the whole situation to a head was a letter from Florea's teacher asking Mrs. Low to come to the school and discuss her daughter's performance in class, which was not up to her usual high standard.

If anything on earth showed that something was not quite right with Florea, it was this.

Florea's assistant principal, Mr. Woodham, was almost as worried as Mrs. Low about what was happening to Florea, especially considering the amount of time she was having to take off because of illness, but he had slightly different theories as to the possible reasons for it. This is often the case with teachers, as they have a habit of seeing children in a totally different light from their parents. There are times when they could be talking about different people altogether.

"You say she's wandering off after school, Mrs. Low," he said, peering intently across his half-glasses. "That suggests secret meetings to me. A boyfriend, perhaps?"

"I think if Florea had a boyfriend, Mr. Woodham, she wouldn't be afraid to tell me. It's not as if her father or I have ever discouraged her from seeing boys. We'd rather welcome it, in fact. I think all children need distractions of some kind in their life. It's not as if school should mean everything to them."

Mr. Woodham cleared his throat and

blinked a couple of times over this last statement. Since school meant everything to him, he pretty much expected everyone else to think the same.

"What I'm going to do, Mrs. Low, until we've sorted out just what's been happening to Florea's scholastic abilities, is to provide a few extra lessons so she's keeping up with the rest of the class. Hopefully, whatever is distracting her from her studies is only a short-term thing, a phase, and she'll be over it soon. In the meantime, an extra tutoring session or two after school hours will make sure she doesn't get too far behind."

"After school?"

"Yes. Every Monday, Wednesday, and Friday. That should be enough."

"If you think that's best."

"Oh, I do, Mrs. Low, I do."

*   *   *

Florea threw a fit when her teacher told her she'd be staying after school three days a week.

She was okay to begin with, accepting the decision in the usual way she accepted things that were beyond her control, but as the day wore on and it got closer and closer to the time she'd usually wander off and disappear for a couple of hours, Florea became very distracted. She spent a lot of time staring out the window, her eyes focused on something far in the distance. When her teacher tried to call her attention back, Florea would fly into a rage of sorts, snapping and arguing about anything that took her fancy. There would be a strange light in her eyes, almost as if something else were looking out of them, something with an angry intelligence that would not accept any interference with its plans.

Even her classmates were saying that Florea had changed and that she wasn't as easy to get along with anymore.

When the final bell of the day rang, Florea leaped from her seat and made a dash for the door, only to run smack bang into Mr. Woodham, who had come to ensure that she made it to her tutoring session. Without even hesitating, she lashed out with her foot and caught him full on the shin with the edge of her boot, causing him to shriek in a high, almost animal way and to hop around on one foot.

While he was doing this, though, he held grimly on to Florea with one arm.

"I don't know what it is you're up to, young lady, but you'll be attending these sessions whether you like it or not. Whoever it is you've got waiting for you outside school will just have to wait their turn."

Florea's eyes looked like they were about to pop right out of her head with frustration.

She opened her mouth and kept on opening it until it looked like a huge black hole in the center of her face, then let fly with a scream filled with such venom that Mr. Woodham very nearly let her go out of sheer fright. She thrashed about, screaming and kicking, her eyes rolling wildly as her classmates eased themselves past in order to go home. This was definitely not the Florea they'd known for the last few years.

Suddenly, she stopped.

For a couple of seconds she sat with her head between her hands while Mr. Woodham and her teacher stood looking suspiciously at her. She shook her head and looked around.

"What's going on?" Florea asked in a quiet little voice.

"That's just what I'd like to know," Mr. Woodham replied.

Florea got up off the ground and brushed

herself off. "I must have fallen over," she said sheepishly.

Mr. Woodham just rubbed his shin and stared at her.

"I suppose I'd better get to my tutoring session," Florea muttered. "I must be late for it by now."

Mr. Woodham was good enough to give Florea a lift home after the tutoring session. In the car he inquired about her outburst outside the classroom, but all Florea could do was look at him blankly. She had no recollection whatsoever of the incident and was quite disturbed when Mr. Woodham rolled up his pants leg to show her the bruise she'd inflicted on his shin.

"It must have been an accident, sir," she muttered, a deep frown on her face. "There's no way I'd kick you deliberately."

Mr. Woodham resolved to talk to Florea's

mother about a session with a psychologist, something he could arrange through the school.

That night Florea ate a normal-sized dinner, slept well, and was more like her usual self at school the next day.

Until the afternoon, that is, when she started to get that look in her eyes.

5 CHAPTER FIVE

There are days in Knox when a dry wind whips itself up into a frenzy way out in the desert somewhere, and after it has finished tearing up the bushes and terrifying everything from tiny lizards to large mammals, it turns its attention on the town.

It screams in from out beyond the edges of the farmland, its face a mottled red cloud seething with fury, and rips up and down the streets, flinging rubbish and leaves and small pets willy-nilly through the air.

The people of Knox are well aware of these winds and, as long as they get enough warning, make sure that the town is locked up and that towels are wedged under doors and windows shut tight to stop the intrusion of fine red dust into their houses. If they don't do this, and the dust gets inside, for days afterward every time they blow their nose it looks as if their brains have exploded, because their handkerchiefs are filled with chunky red mucus.

And it was through one of these winds that the figure of Florea Low staggered, her backpack on her shoulders, face grimly set, toward the old Dixon house.

There had been a warning broadcast over the school PA before the students left for the day, telling them to immediately make their way home before the storm really set in, and in most cases that's exactly what they did. But Florea never heard the warning or, if she did, she'd chosen to ignore it, because the moment that school was out she headed in exactly the opposite direction of where she should have gone.

It was as if she were driven by something much stronger than herself, something that had a hold of her so tightly she was completely unaware of it. All she could hear was that warm, comforting voice pulling her toward the house on the edge of town and the old woman who wanted to talk.

By the time the storm had reached its peak, Mrs. Low was frantic. There was no sign of her daughter, and today was not one of the days she should be staying behind for extra tutoring sessions.

All she could see when she tried to peer out of the windows was swirling red dust and the occasional car crawling along the street. It was as if Florea had been eaten by the landscape.

She thought of calling her husband, but he was in Brisbane ordering supplies for their restaurant and there wasn't a whole lot he'd be able to do from there except worry, and Mrs. Low was already doing more than enough worrying for the two of them.

A call to the school brought no response, which meant that it had been locked up in preparation for the storm. Everyone would have left there hours ago.

Tying a hat to her head with a shawl and donning a pair of her husband's welding glasses to stop the dust from getting into her eyes, Mrs. Low squeezed out through the door and into the storm. It immediately tore at her clothes, wrapping her dress around her legs so tightly it made her look something like a mermaid, and flung her roughly this way and that.

She made a strange but determined figure trudging through the clouds of dust, peering this way and that in search of Florea. But even though she looked under every bush and behind every tree between her house and Florea's school, no sign of her daughter was to be found. Exhausted by the struggle against the wind, she sat in the shelter of the school wall and tried to think of what might have happened, and as she thought, an uncomfortable feeling began to creep slowly up her spine. It was as if a memory — the memory of something better left forgotten — was niggling at the edges of her mind, urging her to slip back in time, to become, for just a short time, a child again, to unearth and look clearly at something she had filed away as just another childhood fantasy.

That was when she heard the voice, far off and fractured by the wind, but still warm and inviting, thick like honey. And the memory of it was so strong, she vomited in a long, hot gush between her feet.

Florea was slumped in a chair on the porch, her eyes rolled back in her head and her legs vibrating rhythmically on the boards. Her mouth was slightly open and a long string of drool ran from the corner of her mouth onto her blouse, where it formed a large, dark splotch. One of her arms was hanging limply down the side of her chair while the other was gripped so tightly in Mrs. Dixon's claw it looked as if she'd sunk her fingers deep into Florea's flesh. Only her hand didn't really look like a claw anymore, rather more like the hand of someone of forty or so, filled out and plump, with a slight pink tinge to it. She was leaning across and whispering into Florea's ear, and as she talked, it appeared that Mrs. Dixon was filling out, growing little by little. You could almost see the blood pumping through the veins in her face, pulsing under her skin, which seemed to billow and move as if pushed from inside. The very wrinkles in her face were disappearing almost by magic.

But the thing about Mrs. Dixon that was most alive was her eyes, which glittered like tiny diamonds, hard and evil and as cold as black ice.

When Mrs. Low finally found her, Florea was staggering through the storm about a hundred yards from the old house at the edge of town, her hair in disarray and her backpack dangling loosely from her hand. She was being tossed about by the wind, buffeted this way and that, but didn't really seem to notice. Her eyes were glassy and she had a slight, faraway smile on her face. It took Florea a few seconds to recognize her mother, which was understandable considering the welding glasses and hat tied to Mrs. Low's head.

"You've been at that house, haven't you?" Mrs. Low screamed through the howling of the wind. "You've been with that old woman, the witch, haven't you?"

Florea looked puzzled.

"I've just been wandering around thinking, Mom," she slurred. "I've been having all these wonderful thoughts about faraway places and beautiful buildings and strange, interesting people."

As Mrs. Low dragged Florea off down the street in the direction of their home, she looked back at the old house and was sure that, just for a second (or it may have just been a trick of the storm), she saw a figure standing at the rusted gate surrounded by swirling dust and leaves. A figure that raised its hand and waved.

But when Mrs. Low looked again, there was nothing there except a rusted gate hanging from a bluestone wall.

CHAPTER SIX

This time Mrs. Low didn't worry about calling a doctor for Florea. Instead, she simply put her to bed and sat there watching as her daughter drifted off into an unsettled, sweaty sleep. She wiped her brow with a cold washcloth and looked at her tired, drawn features. Florea had quite obviously lost weight, and you could see tiny wrinkles forming at the edges of her eyes and mouth.

It was almost as if she were slowly drying up, all the youth being sucked out of her.

When Florea was deeply asleep, Mrs. Low quietly rose and walked down the corridor of their house to the small room at the back where they stored many of the more exotic ingredients her husband used when he cooked some of his famous dishes in the restaurant.

Stacked around the walls of the room and piled on shelves were sacks filled with strange dried fungi, rare herbs and spices, odd-shaped bits of bark, and things that may or may not have once been parts of animals and fish. Slowly she went from sack to sack, taking a bit from here and a bit from there and collecting them all in a heavy stone bowl.

When she had everything she thought she needed, Mrs. Low then took an old book down from the very top shelf in the storeroom, flicked through the pages of ancient, handwritten Chinese script until she found the section she was after, and carefully checked off the ingredients against what was written in the book. A couple of times she went back to the shelves and added various things to the bowl, and when she was satisfied she had everything she needed, took up the stone pestle and began to grind the ingredients down to a fine powder.

As she worked, she chanted softly to herself, remembering words she thought she'd forgotten, words that were so ancient even Mrs. Low had no idea what they meant.

When the powder was ready, she tipped it carefully into a square of brown paper, folded it, took an odd-shaped clay kettle from a shelf, and moved out of the storeroom and into the kitchen. She filled the kettle almost to the top with water, poured in the powder, tapping the paper to make sure that every bit had gone into the kettle, lit the gas jet on the stove, turned the heat down to its lowest possible level, and placed the kettle above the tiny flame.

Then she went back into Florea's bedroom and spent the rest of the night wiping her daughter's brow.

During the night, while she sat in an armchair next to her daughter's bed, Mrs. Low drifted in and out of an uncomfortable half sleep; her head slowly settling onto the back of the chair and then suddenly snapping forward as she realized she was dropping off. In these periods of being not-quite-conscious, Mrs. Low dreamed of her own childhood in Knox, back in the fifties, when life was a little slower and her own mother had warned her about the house at the edge of town and the old woman whom she referred to in Chinese as a ghost.

Like Florea, Mrs. Low had been a little more than just curious about the story. She clearly remembered visiting the house the first time, walking up the path and finding old Mrs. Dixon in the chair on the porch, but after that it had become blurred. Though she remembered, deep down inside her, a voice that seemed to glow, to fill her with wonderful sensations and beautiful thoughts, a voice that was like a drug, taking away all thought of anything except the desire to listen, to be lulled, enfolded within its caress. She couldn't remember exactly what the voice had said, just the sensation of it flowing through her. She couldn't remember anything except for one phrase: Talk to me.

For many years after that time, Mrs. Low could not remember anything more, but she knew that she had been sick for quite some time after, and her parents, steeped as they were in the traditions they had brought from their country, had been very worried.

Eventually, she recovered, but not until her mother had taken matters into her own hands. Unfortunately for Mrs. Low, her mother and father had not gone into detail about what exactly happened or what they'd done to remedy the situation. And from that time on they'd spent all their time ensuring that their daughter became more Australian than the Australians she was living among.

Before she died, however, Mrs. Low's mother had finally decided to pass on some of the things she knew about herbs and traditional medicines, including how to use the remedies contained in the old book she'd brought from China. Mrs. Low, however, had never had cause to use any of them until now.

She hoped she'd got the right one. For Florea's sake, she hoped she knew what she was doing.

*　　*　　*

When Florea awoke in the morning, her eyes were gummy and her tongue a sickly white color. Her breath smelled like a sewer and you could hear mucus in her chest.

Mrs. Low was not at all surprised when Florea could not remember where she had been the afternoon before and, after making sure that she was comfortable in her bed, went out and called the school to say that her daughter would be ill again that day.

Mr. Woodham was not pleased, but Florea's mother told him, rather abruptly, that as far as she was concerned her daughter's health was all that mattered to her and another day away from school was not going to make all that much difference in the scheme of things. Then she hung up the phone so loudly it almost blew out one of his eardrums.

On the way back to Florea's bedroom,

63

Mrs. Low took the kettle, which had been simmering on the stove all night, and poured the concoction into a tiny porcelain teacup. What came out of the spout looked like black tar and it smelled pretty much like it looked. She dipped her finger into it and placed a tiny bit on the end of her tongue, screwing up her face as she did.

"Ugh," she said. "Anything this foul has to be good for you."

Back in Florea's bedroom, she sat her daughter up and plumped up the pillows behind her.

"Here," she said, holding the tiny cup up to Florea's mouth, "swallow this really quickly and try not to breathe while you do it."

The sticky liquid was in Florea's mouth before she really knew what was happening, but as soon as she had a taste of it her eyes opened with an expression of total horror.

Immediately, Mrs. Low grabbed Florea's nose, pinching it tight, so all her daughter could do was swallow. As soon as she did, however, she started gagging loudly.

"What are you trying to do to me, Mom?" she shrieked as soon as she could get her breath back. "You're trying to poison me, aren't you! You think I'm faking being sick and that this is going to make me go to school! Well, I am sick. I really am."

"I know, dear."

"By the way, what's for breakfast?"

"Anything you want, dear."

"Steak and eggs? Oh, gag me with a spoon, that tastes horrible."

"I know, it's meant to."

That day, Florea ate like a soccer team after a World Cup match, consuming over a dozen eggs, a couple of good-sized steaks, a gigantic bowl of garlic-and-parsley pasta, chocolate pudding, five apples, an orange, seven tangerines, an entire pack of Pop-Tarts, some bacon, and a plate of stir-fried vegetables and rice.

"Still hungry, dear?" her mother asked after dinner.

"Maybe some peanuts?" Florea replied. "I don't know what's wrong with me. There still seems to be this little area in my stomach that just doesn't seem to ever get filled up."

She gave a little shiver after she said this, as if someone or something had just walked over her grave.

"I understand, dear," her mother said, rubbing her back affectionately. "You just eat as much as you want to. Get your strength back. I'm going to keep you away from school again tomorrow, just to make sure you're feeling in tip-top condition."

"But I'm not feeling all that bad now, Mom. I'll be okay for school. I mean, I've missed so much of it lately. I don't want to fall too far behind. And that vile stuff you gave me seems to have cleared up the cold or whatever it was that I had."

"You'll be staying home again tomorrow, whether you're feeling well or not. There's no discussion on that matter," her mother said as she went out to fill the bowl with peanuts.

Florea shrugged her shoulders. Her mother had always insisted that she keep up with her schoolwork, but she wasn't going to argue the point. If she wanted her to have another day off, so be it. She just hoped that her mother didn't want her to drink any more of that mixture she'd had that morning.

7

CHAPTER SEVEN

The next day Florea spent wandering around the house, complaining that she was as fit as a fiddle and there was no reason she shouldn't go back to school.

Her mother quietly insisted otherwise and eventually Florea accepted the situation.

That was until the afternoon, when Florea's eyes got a faraway look and she began to spend a lot of time staring out the window and shuffling about restlessly.

"Something the matter, dear?" her mother asked.

"I think I might go out for a walk," Florea replied in a strangely disembodied voice.

"Whatever you like," her mother replied.

When Florea walked out the door, her mother followed about fifty yards behind.

As Mrs. Low expected, Florea headed straight for the old Dixon house, neither looking right nor left. She walked straight in through the rusted gate and disappeared up the path.

Mrs. Low waited in the street outside, hoping that she'd done everything right. Hoping that she'd remembered what her mother had taught her.

When Florea sat in the chair on the porch, old Mrs. Dixon smiled and reached out to hold her arm. Though it would be difficult to call Mrs. Dixon "old" anymore. Her face had hardly any wrinkles on it and she seemed to be so full of life that she literally glowed pink. Her hair had developed a definite auburn color and there was a lot more flesh on her bones.

Florea, on the other hand, seemed to shrivel up the closer Mrs. Dixon came.

"Talk to me, dear," she said as her hand closed around Florea's arm.

What happened next was quite bizarre.

As Mrs. Dixon's hand gripped Florea, both of them gave out a loud grunt of surprise, and both their eyes opened wide.

The glazed look in Florea's eyes immediately disappeared, to be replaced by one of horror. It was as if she'd never seen Mrs. Dixon before, and to find her there holding her arm was as alarming as it was unpleasant.

As for Mrs. Dixon, she was trying like mad to tear her hand away, but it seemed to be stuck to Florea. She opened her mouth wide and let fly with an awesome shriek that was so terrifying it made Florea's hair stand on end.

Mrs. Dixon started to shudder madly, vibrating like a computer game gone totally out of control, her mouth opening and closing and her teeth chattering inside peeled-back gums.

While Florea tried to pull away from the horror that was holding her, Mrs. Dixon seemed to shrivel before her very eyes, as if the flesh were being sucked out of her. Wrinkles began to appear on her face and hands, and the color disappeared from her hair. She flapped about, writhing and screaming, while Florea tried desperately to pull away.

Suddenly, Florea's arms came free, and she leaped from the porch and sprinted down the path for the gate. Looking back once over her shoulder she saw a shriveled bundle collapsed in one of the wicker chairs, one arm stretched out desperately toward her, and she thought she heard a voice calling, "Talk to me" as she bolted through the gate.

Outside Florea was surprised to find her mother waiting with open arms. As she collapsed into her embrace, her mother whispered, "Welcome home, dear."

Florea had never felt so welcome anywhere in her life.

And from that time on, she never went close to the old house at the far end of town, though for the life of her she could never remember why.

S.R. MARTIN

S.R. Martin was born and grew up in the beachside suburbs of Perth, Australia. A fascination with the ocean led to an early career in marine biology, but this was cut short when he decided the specimens he collected looked better under an orange-and-cognac sauce than they did under a microscope. After even quicker careers in banking, teaching, and journalism, a wanderlust led him through most of Australia's capital cities and then on to periods of time living in Hong Kong, Taiwan, South Korea, the United Kingdom, and the United States. Returning to Australia, he settled for Melbourne and a career as a freelance writer. In addition to the Insomniacs series, S.R. Martin is the author of *Swampland*, coming soon from Scholastic.